Emma's Turtle

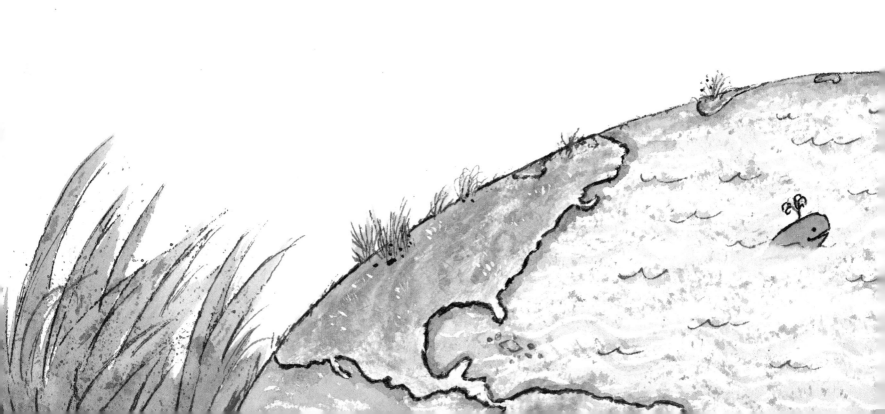

Emma's Turtle

Eve Bunting • Illustrated by **Marsha Winborn**

BOYDS MILLS PRESS
AN IMPRINT OF HIGHLIGHTS
Honesdale, Pennsylvania

Boyds Mills Press
An Imprint of Highlights
815 Church Street
Honesdale, Pennsylvania 18431
Printed in China

Library of Congress Cataloging-in-Publication Data

Bunting, Eve.
  Emma's turtle / Eve Bunting ; illustrated by Marsha Winborn.—1st ed.
    p. cm.
  Summary: When Emma's box turtle digs his way out of his pen, he imagines that he is having
    adventures in Africa, India, and other faraway lands that Emma has described to him.
  ISBN: 978-1-59078-350-4 (hc) • 978-1-62091-735-0 (pb)
  [1. Adventure and adventurers—Fiction. 2. Box turtle—Fiction. 3. Turtles—Fiction.]
  I. Winborn, Marsha, ill. II. Title.

  PZ7.B91527Ens 2007
  [E]—dc22
                              2006037938

First paperback edition, 2014
The text of this book is set in Minion.
The illustrations are done in watercolor.

10 9 8 7 6 5 4 3 2 1

For Coconut, Hazel, and Pineapple: turtles all!

—EB

I am Emma's turtle.

I live in a pen in her backyard. Emma visits me often
and brings me snacks. I let her stroke my head.

She sits in her swing and reads to me of the world and places that are far, far away. She shows me pictures of elephants in Africa and kangaroos in Australia. There are tigers in India and panda bears in China. It is all quite amazing.

My life is good. But I often dream of the world that is far, far away.

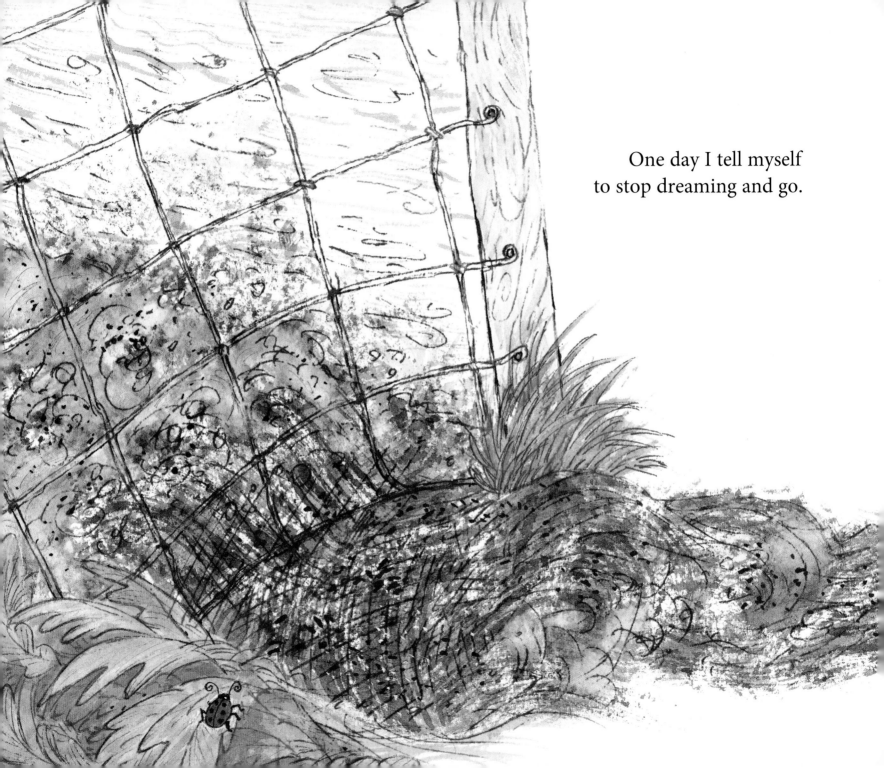

One day I tell myself
to stop dreaming and go.

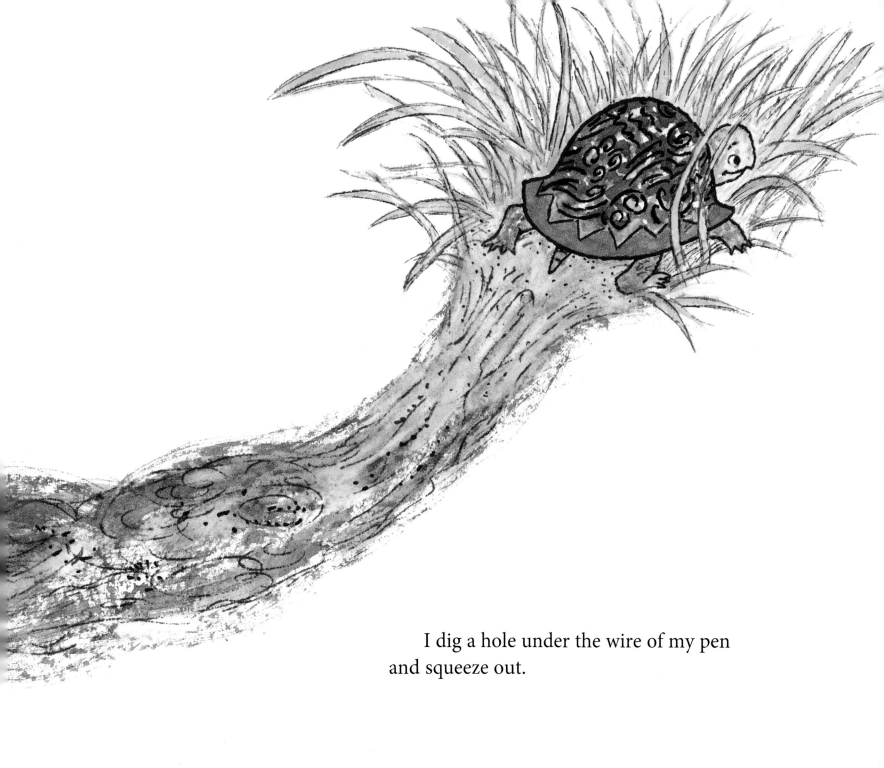

I dig a hole under the wire of my pen
and squeeze out.

I am walking in this place I've never
walked before.
  My legs are short and the grass is long.
I think this must be a jungle.

Perhaps I am in Africa. Is that an elephant leg in front of me? Oh, I am going to be squished! No, it is the stump of some strange jungle tree.

I plod on.

I have come so far now that I think this must be Australia. Is that a kangaroo leaping through the grassland? No, it's a frog. But since it is an Australian frog, it is very interesting. Frogs certainly move fast.

I hear bells chime. Ah, they must be temple bells
and this must be India.

Yikes! Is that a tiger?

I pull my two shells together so he can't eat me.
But when I peep out, I see it is just the silly striped cat
from next door. I never knew he sometimes visited India.

An Indian beetle watches me. He looks exactly like other beetles I have known. We are eyes-to-eyes.

"It's nice here in India," I tell him. "But come visit me in the United States. It is nice there, too."

"I may do that," he says.

I gaze around. "Do you know where the United States is from here?" I ask.

"Sorry," he says and crawls off.

I am worried. I have come so far. Will I be able to find my way home? Will I have to stay in India forever?

A voice is calling.

"Turtle? Turtle? Where are you?"

Hooray! It's my Emma!

"I am here in India," I say. But I am
using Turtle Talk and she doesn't understand.
She sees me and picks me up.
"Thank goodness I found you."

Thank goodness.

It is so good to be off my feet. I let her stroke my head.
She has brought a snail for me in her pocket. It is fat
and juicy and splendid.

Emma carries me back and sets me in my pen.
Strawberry slices are scattered about for my supper.
I am tired. But I can still eat.

Emma leans across my wire fence.

"Poor Turtle," she croons. "I bet it took you all day to go from one end of our yard to the other. I hope it was exciting for you."

Did I really go only from one end of the yard to the other?

Astonishing!

Still, it is exciting to have the whole world
here in my backyard.
I settle to sleep. A traveling turtle needs his rest.
Tomorrow I will dig another hole.
I need to go again and find China.